Bold Words

by M.G. Higgins

SADDLEBACK
EDUCATIONAL PUBLISHING
www.sdlback.com

All source images from Shutterstock.com

ISBN-13: 978-1-68021-159-7
ISBN-10: 1-68021-159-5
eBook: 978-1-63078-467-6

Printed in Malaysia

21 20 19 18 17   1 2 3 4 5

Loud machines clank. Dust fills my nose. The heat reminds me of the farm. But this heat is stuffy.

My mind wanders. Thoughts of late summer harvests fill my head.

"Flo!" a voice yells. "Stop dreaming!"

The foreman is speaking to me. I nod and turn back to my machine. The loom is what turns thread into cloth.

I lace a thread through the harnesses.
Then I start the machine.

Clunk, clunk.

One harness rises. The other harness
lowers. The shuttle with thread passes
between them.

Clunk, clunk.

The day goes by slowly. My shift is twelve hours long. There are two more hours to go. I try not to think about time.

I hear a scream. It is Molly. She is at the loom next to mine.

"My hand!" Molly cries. "It's caught!"

Oh no! I run over and turn off the loom.

"Get back to work," the foreman yells.

Molly cries out in pain. Her hand is still trapped. My stomach turns. Her bones must be crushed.

The foreman tries to help her. He stops to glare at me. "This is your last warning," he says.

There is nothing I can do. I return to my loom.

Molly holds her broken hand. She cries as she leaves the building.

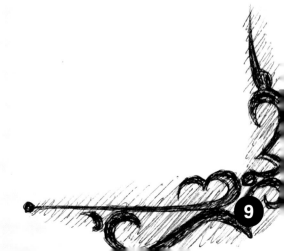

My shift **finally** ends. I walk with other girls to the boarding house. Some of them talk about Molly.

"What will she do?" Sarah asks. "She can't work at the mill."

"She has a brother," Ann says.
"Maybe he'll take her in."

It is hard to sleep that night.
I'm thinking about my job. The
conditions are so bad. I would like
to quit. But how would I live? There
is no one to take me in.

My parents died from the flu.
Typhoid killed my brother. Then the
bank took the farm.

There is only my sister, Isabel. She is a maid. Her pay is even **lower** than mine. I toss and turn all night.

The morning bell rings. It is hard to wake up. I barely slept. But my shift begins soon. So I quickly get ready and run to the mill.

I sit at my loom and begin working. The cloth I'm weaving is green. *It would make a lovely dress,* I think.

Soon the cloth is ready to come off the loom. I lift the heavy roll of fabric. It slips from my fingers and slides across the loom.

Now the cloth is covered with grease. It falls and unrolls across the dirty floor. The cloth is **ruined**.

The foreman runs over. He looks at the cloth then at me. "You're fired, Flo!" he shouts.

I gasp. "No, please. It won't happen again. I'm a good worker."

"You're a **daydreamer**," he says. "I've got ten girls waiting to replace you."

My mouth opens to speak. There is so much I want to say. The looms are not safe. We work too many hours. Everyone is tired. But it's **useless**. Nothing I say will make a difference.

All I can do is collect my pay and leave. Then I walk to the boarding house and pack.

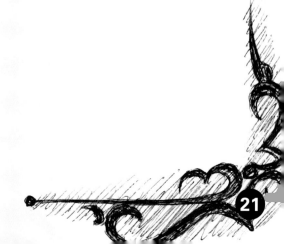

One thing is sure. The money I have **saved** will not last long. Maybe my sister can help. She might know a family that needs a maid.

Isabel lives far away. It will take all day to get there. I begin the long walk.

Finally, I reach the business section of town. My feet hurt and I'm **tired**. So I stop to rest.

There is a building with signs on it. Like many women I know, I didn't go to school. But I can read. Mother taught me.

Sometimes I think about having a different kind of life. School would have changed everything. Maybe I could have been a nurse or a teacher. Life would be easier.

One sign catches my eye. There is a picture of a machine. It has rows of buttons. Each button is labeled with a letter.

Words on the sign read, "The Remington Typewriter. Learn to type! Get an office job!"

Type? I don't know what that means. But an office job sounds good. Middle-class people work in offices. It is better than being a **laborer**.

An address is listed on the sign. The place is a few blocks away. I hurry down the street.

The building is just ahead. When I get there, I stop to catch my breath. Then I go inside.

A young man sits behind a desk.
"Can I help you?" he asks.

"I want to **learn** to type," I say.

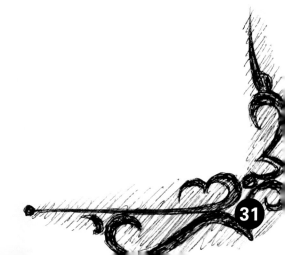

The man looks me up and down. Suddenly I'm embarrassed. My clothes are **ragged**. Maybe he thinks I'm not good enough.

"Can you read?" he asks.

"Yes," I say.

He tells me about the class. Those who pass can get a job typing.

Then he tells me how much the class costs. My shoulders **sag**. It is more than I can afford. "I'm sorry I bothered you," I say.

This was a silly idea. I'm only meant to be a laborer.

"Wait," the man says.

I turn to face him.

"We have a program," he says. "Take the class now. Pay for it when you get a job. The fee is taken from your wages. Are you interested?"

"Yes!" I say.

The class starts tomorrow. First, I need somewhere to live. My sister's place is too small. But this gives me an idea. We can rent a room together.

I finally arrive at my sister's place. Isabel is happy to see me. She likes my idea. We find a room that is **cheap**. That night I sleep well.

It is early the next morning. I'm the first one at school. Soon the room fills with other women. The lesson begins.

Mr. Jones is our teacher. He explains how to type. "Place your fingers on the keys in the middle row. Tap keys with your fingers. Try not to look at your hands."

At first it is confusing. My fingers don't move very fast. But with practice, I **memorize** the keys.

Two weeks go by. My typing has improved. I make very few mistakes.

Mr. Jones gives us a typing test. He tells me I passed. "You can join the group of typists."

This is **good** news. My money has run out.

I begin working the next day. The job is at a busy law office. There is a lot of typing to do.

Work starts at 8:00 AM. There is a thirty-minute break for lunch. My shift ends at 5:30. I can't **believe** it.

That is only nine hours of work. And the office is closed on Saturdays and Sundays. I get both days off.

The work is safe. It's not hard to breathe. Workers are treated well. No one yells. The lawyers are polite. They call me by my last name—Miss James.

On Friday, I get my first paycheck. Money has been taken out for the typing class. But there is enough left for rent and food.

A few weeks go by. I have gotten to know the other typists. Most are women. Two are men.

One woman becomes a friend. Her name is Sally. We meet every day in the lunchroom.

Today Sally seems upset. She slams her cup on the table.

"What's wrong?" I ask.

"I saw a letter," she says. "It listed how much the typists make. The men make **twice** as much as we do!"

"Of course," I say. "They are men."

"But we do the same work," she says. "We should be paid the same."

A woman named Liz laughs.
"Are you ranting about fairness
again?"

"Yes, and why not?" Sally says.
"Women have no power. If only
we could vote. Things would
change."

"Keep dreaming," Liz says.

"I'm not dreaming," Sally says.
"I'm doing something about it."

"What do you mean?" I ask.

"I'm a **suffragette**."

I know the term. A suffragette is someone who fights for women's rights. That includes the right to vote.

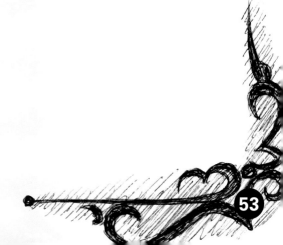

"Do you think women will ever get to vote?" I ask.

"Count on it," Sally says. "Are you interested in joining us?"

"Oh, I don't think so."

We finish lunch and go back to work.

I glance at Sally. She behaves differently in the office. Here she is quiet. Her actions are professional.

In the lunchroom, she is bold. She lets her emotions show. Sally has strong opinions. It's what I like most about her.

One weekend, Sally invites me to see where she lives. She calls it a **settlement house**. People in the community come here for different services.

We step inside. Sally stops at a doorway. I peek into the room. Young children are gathered. A woman reads to them.

"That's the day care," Sally whispers. "Some girls babysit for single mothers who work."

We pass another room. It's filled with rows of chairs.

"That's the meeting room," Sally says. "We teach English to immigrants. And we give talks on important topics. Health concerns. Local issues."

"Who is in charge?" I ask.

"The women who own the house. They live here too," Sally says.

"Don't they have families?" I ask.

"Yes. But they are **independent**."

"But men are involved, right?" I ask.

"Just women," Sally says.

This is amazing. It's something I want to be part of.

Sally puts me to work typing. I also attend a talk.

A woman named Clara is the speaker. She talks about ways women are treated **unfairly**. They are not treated equally in the workplace.

This is something I can relate to. I raise my hand to speak. The group **listens** to my stories about the mill. "It's a hopeless cause," I tell them.

Clara smiles. "Not true. Change is possible," she says.

"How?" I ask.

"Join us," Clara says. "We're starting a trade union for women. Help us organize a strike."

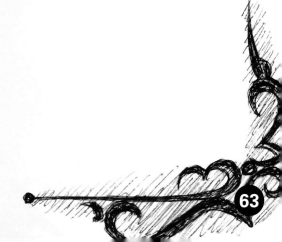

A strike? The idea scares me. It would take courage to speak out. Would I be punished for it?

Then I consider how far I have come. My life is so much better now.

Yes, I decide. *Things must change. And I can help make it happen.*

TEEN EMERGENT READER LIBRARIES®

BOOSTERS

The Literacy Revolution Continues with New TERL
Booster Titles! *Each Sold Individually*

9781680211290

9781680211535

9781680211313

ENGAGE [2]

EXCEL [3]

9781680214871

9781680211580

9781680214888

9781680211306

9781680211320

9781680214604

9781680211597

9781680214635

9781680214864

SOAR [4]

[TERL]

TEEN EMERGENT
READER LIBRARIES®

[1]
EMERGE

9781622508662

[2]
ENGAGE

9781622508679

[3]
EXCEL

9781622508686

[4]
SOAR

9781680213041

www.jointheliteracyrevolution.com